"TAP-DANCIN' ON COW PIES!"

That's what Farmer Ben thinks of the cubs' idea to hold a Halloween Festival to help save his failing family farm. After all, no self-respecting farmer would turn his place into a Theme Park!

Then a couple of Ben's long-dead ancestors pay him a little visit. Will Ben's farm go bust? Or will the ghostly forebears come to the rescue in the nick of time?

The Berenstain Bears and the HAUNTED HAYRIDE

by the Berenstains

A BIG CHAPTER BOOK™

Random House New York

http://www.randomhouse.com/

Library of Congress Cataloging-in-Publication Data
Berenstain, Stan, 1923-
The Berenstain Bears' haunted hayride / by the Berenstains.
   p. cm. — (A Big chapter book)
SUMMARY: Farmer Ben takes a dim view of the cubs' plan to hold a Hal-
loween Festival to help save his floundering family farm, and the situation
is complicated when a couple of Ben's dead ancestors show up.
ISBN 0-679-87650-2 (trade). — ISBN 0-679-97650-7 (lib. bdg.)
[1. Halloween—Fiction.   2. Ghosts—Fiction.   3. Farms—Fiction.
4. Bears—Fiction.]   I. Berenstain, Jan, 1923- .   II. Title.
III. Series: Berenstain, Stan, 1923-   Big chapter book.
PZ7.B4483Berhe   1997
[Fic]—dc21
96-52541

Printed in the United States of America 10 9 8 7 6 5 4 3 2 1

BIG CHAPTER BOOKS is a trademark of Berenstain Enterprises, Inc.

Contents

Chapter 1
Job Hunt

Brother Bear's great idea didn't just come out of nowhere. It came out of something Lizzy Bruin said as the cubs walked home from school one day in early fall.

As the cubs walked, they complained about their money problems. Every year, in late September, the cubs started saving money from their allowances to buy costumes for Halloween. And the moment

Halloween was over, they had to start saving all over again for Christmas. Christmas gifts for family members could be quite expensive. That meant no movies at the mall multiplex, no shakes at the Burger Bear, and no video games at the arcade from Halloween to Christmas.

"Here we go again," groused Queenie McBear. "First we get squeezed by Halloween, and then we get totally *crushed* by Christmas."

"Bummer," said Barry Bruin.

"Yeah," agreed his sister Lizzy. "But what can we do? Our allowances are the only money we have."

That's what gave Brother his idea. "I know what we can do," he said. "Instead of complaining, like we do every year, we can get jobs. That way we'll have our allowances *and* our wages."

"That's a great idea!" said Babs Bruno. "But who would hire us? We're just a bunch of cubs."

Brother was quick to point out that several of them had parents or other relatives who owned businesses. Papa Q. Bear, for example, had a successful carpentry business. Lizzy and Barry's father owned Biff

Bruin's Pharmacy. And then there was Squire Grizzly, Bonnie Brown's uncle. The squire owned Great Grizzly National Bank, the Burger Bear chain, and a half-dozen other Beartown businesses. Bonnie was away, traveling with a musical show, so she couldn't ask her uncle for help. But Squire Grizzly had long been Papa Bear's best customer. Brother could ask Papa to telephone the squire about their job hunt.

Most of the cubs thought it would be cool to work at the Burger Bear, their favorite after-school hangout. But Ferdy Factual had his heart set on being a research assistant for his uncle Actual Factual at the Bearsonian Institution.

After dinner, the cubs gathered at the Burger Bear, where they had agreed to meet to celebrate their new jobs. Brother and Sister were late, but the others didn't have to worry about waiting for them to start the celebration. That's because there were no jobs to celebrate.

"What a letdown," Barry was saying. "My dad says business isn't so good right now. He can't afford to hire anyone. Not even cubs."

"I'm afraid the Bearsonian won't be of any assistance, either," said Ferdy. "Uncle Actual says it runs on donations from Bear Country businesses. Lately a lot of busi-

nesses have been doing poorly, so donations are down. He *will* take us on as volunteers, however."

"Oh, great!" said Queenie. "That'll be a *big* help!"

Ferdy shrugged. "It would keep us out of trouble, at least," he said. "Away from the mall and the arcade and *this* place."

"You just like all that science stuff!" snapped Queenie. "You don't even really want a job!"

"Chill out, Queenie," said Cousin Fred. "Here come Brother and Sister. And they're both smiling."

Indeed they were. With big grins on their faces, Brother and Sister slid into the booth and ordered shakes.

"So, tell us the good news!" said Babs. "What did your dad say?"

"He's been working alone for so many

years," said Brother, "that he wouldn't have the slightest idea how to use any assistants."

"Then he must have asked Squire Grizzly to hire us," said Trudy. "So, where are we working? Here or the bank?"

Still grinning, Brother and Sister shook their heads.

"Neither?" Queenie said. "Then why in the world are you two sitting there with those silly grins on your faces?"

"Just as Papa was about to pick up the phone to call Squire Grizzly," Brother explained, "Farmer Ben called about an oak table Papa's repairing for him. They got to talking, and Ben told Papa that the farm has run into hard times. He had to fire his full-time farm hand. And now a lot of chores aren't getting done. So Papa asked him if he would hire us to do them. And he said yes!"

"Super!" cried Babs.

"Outta sight!" said Queenie.

"How much is he gonna pay us?" asked Lizzy.

"Not much," said Brother. "Just chicken feed."

"*Chicken feed?*" gasped Barry. "We can't pay for Christmas gifts with *chicken feed!* We'll get kicked out of every store!"

"It's just an expression," said Fred. "It means 'money, but not a lot.' "

"I knew that," said Barry, blushing.

"But that's perfect," said Trudy. "We don't need a lot of money. And Farmer Ben needs help but can't afford to pay high wages. So it's a good deal for us *and* him. I think we should celebrate with another round of shakes. Right, Ferd?" She turned to her boyfriend, then frowned. "What's wrong?" she asked. "You don't look happy."

Ferdy shrugged. "I never look happy," he said.

"But you don't even look your usual bored," said Trudy. "You look upset."

Ferdy folded his arms and looked away. "Well, why shouldn't I be upset?" he said. "*Farmwork?*"

"What's wrong with farmwork?" asked Sister.

"Are you joking?" said Ferdy. "It's dirty. And smelly."

"Oh, gimme a break!" moaned Queenie. "As if you've never done dirty or smelly work before! What about when you helped your uncle study the algae in Great Grizzly Lake and came back every day with your knickers full of muck?"

"Yeah," said Barry. "And what about the time you studied the plants and animals of Forbidden Bog and fell in quicksand?"

"That's different," said Ferdy coldly. "That was *science!*"

Trudy was eyeing Ferdy with suspicion. "I think I know what's *really* bothering you," she said.

"Oh?" said Ferdy. "And what is it, pray tell?"

"You think farmwork is beneath you, don't you?" said Trudy. "You don't think it will challenge your mind."

"Well, how could farmwork possibly challenge the mind of a genius?" Ferdy scoffed.

"Oh, come on, Ferd," said Brother. "Don't knock it till you've tried it. At least give it a chance."

With a sigh, Ferdy unfolded his arms. "All right," he said. "I'll try it. For one day. But if it's boring…"

Chapter 2
A Farmer's Pride

The sun was just beginning to peek over the horizon when the cubs reached the front porch of the Bens' farmhouse the following Saturday. Ferdy let out a yawn as Brother reached up and rang the doorbell. But it wasn't his usual bored yawn. It was a sleepy yawn. And as sleepy yawns have a way of doing, it set off a wave of yawning among the cubs.

"Why in the world did we have to get up while it was still dark?" asked Queenie.

"I heard that!" boomed Farmer Ben's deep voice as the front door swung open. That made the cubs jump, but they relaxed as soon as they saw that he was grinning. "The answer is: to learn how a farmer lives," Ben continued. "A farmer always wakes while it's still dark and gets to work at the crack of dawn." He looked off to the east. "I see that dawn's a-crackin' already. Come in, cubs."

The cubs followed Farmer Ben into the living room, where they sat on a sofa and some chairs.

"Today is just for watching, listening, and

learning," said Farmer Ben. "Next Saturday you'll start doing chores all by yourselves. Before then you'll each need to buy a pair of overalls like mine. Now, any questions before we go outside?"

Sister started to raise her hand, then remembered she wasn't in school. "I have

one, Farmer Ben," she said. She pointed to three portraits that hung on the wall behind Ben. "Who are they?"

"Why, they're my ancestors," said Farmer Ben. "This one on the left is my great-grandfather, Ben Ezra, and the one in the middle is my grandfather, Ben Abner. And the last one is my father, Ben Noah." His eyes got misty as he looked at the portraits of bears in overalls. "This farm has been passed down from father to son for generations," he explained. "I plan to pass it down to my own son, Ben Wilmer, who's studying farm science at Big Bear University. I'm mighty proud of that. We Bens are bears of the land, and we'll never leave it."

Farmer Ben spoke these words with a catch in his voice and a tear in his eye. It was clear to the cubs that he had deep feelings about his farm. But there was something else about his speech. Something troubling.

The cubs were all thinking the same thing, but, as usual, it was Queenie who blurted it out. "Papa Bear said your farm is having hard times and that you had to fire your farm hand," she said. "Is that true?"

The cubs saw a hardness come into Farmer Ben's face. At first they thought he was angry with Queenie for raising the subject. But after a moment he relaxed and said, "It's true, cubs. And it's a darn shame. Jake is a fine farm hand. I hated to let him go. But I had no choice. Mrs. Ben did his chores for a while. But then things got so bad that she had to take a job at the fabric store in town to help support the farm. That's why I've hired you cubs."

"But why have things gotten so bad for the farm?" asked Sister.

Farmer Ben sighed. "It's a long story," he said. "For years and years I've sold my fruits, vegetables, and dairy products to the five grocery stores in the Beartown area. But about six months ago, Ed Hooper opened Hooper's Sooper-Dooper Market out on the highway near Birder's Woods. Maybe some of you have been there."

"I have," said Queenie. "It's huge. And it's got everything."

"That's just the trouble," said Ben. "Hooper's sells everything the small grocery stores sell and more. Plus, it sells everything cheaper. The small stores have lost so many

17

customers to Hooper's that three of them have already gone out of business. That's been real tough on the farm."

"Why is it tough on the farm?" asked Brother. "Can't you sell your goods to Hooper?"

"Oh, I do," said Ben. "But Hooper doesn't pay us farmers nearly as much as the grocery stores do. He claims he can't afford to pay as much because he sells cheap. But I'm not so sure about that."

"Why?" asked Brother.

"Because of what happened when

Hooper opened his first Sooper-Dooper Market over in Bearville," said Ben. "Before that, he was just an ordinary small business-bear with a successful grocery store in Bearville. Then he borrowed a lot of money from some big businessbears in Big Bear City and opened the first Hooper's Sooper-Dooper Market. At first he sold everything cheap. Of course, he lost money because of his low prices. But the loans kept him going until all the other grocery stores went out of business. As soon as Hooper's was the only supermarket left in Bearville, he raised his prices. In fact, he raised them higher than they had been at the small grocery stores. But by then his customers had nowhere else to shop."

"But when Hooper raised his prices," said Brother, "couldn't he also pay farmers more for their goods?"

"He could," said Farmer Ben, "but he didn't. That way he made a huge profit. At first, local farmers refused to sell their goods at such low prices. But Hooper had enough money to pay truckers to bring farm goods in from all over Bear Country. Finally, the local farmers were forced to sell to Hooper. So Hooper and his backers got richer while the farmers and shoppers got poorer."

The cubs were silent for a while after Farmer Ben finished speaking. Finally, Sister asked, "So, what will you do if Hooper tries the same thing here?"

Ben thought for a moment. "I don't know, cubs," he said. "I'm already just hanging on by the skin of my teeth. Some folks

are saying I should sell the farm. And I've had lots of offers from land developers who want to turn it into a housing development or a parking lot or some such thing. But I refuse to sell. The Bens have farmed this land ever since Ben Ezra first plowed, planted, and harvested it. And I just can't let him and my other farmer ancestors down by selling it."

Ben was misty-eyed again as he looked long and hard at the portraits. "But don't worry, cubs," he said, swallowing the lump in his throat. "I'll think of something."

Ben kept staring at the portraits, as though the solution would somehow come from them. And then he said something that made the cubs realize that he really *was* expecting some kind of help from his ancestors.

"I have faith, cubs," said Ben. "Faith in the wisdom of my ancestors. *They* wouldn't let anything happen to this farm. You know, sometimes I feel as if their spirits are still here, protecting the farm."

That gave the cubs a strange, shivery feeling. They looked at one another, wondering what Farmer Ben would say next.

Chapter 3
Farm Hand Ferdy

"All right," said Farmer Ben. "Let's get crackin'."

Just then Ferdy let out a yawn. Farmer Ben smiled and said, "Still sleepy, son?"

"That's not his sleepy yawn," said Trudy, glaring at Ferdy. "That's his bored yawn. He probably won't be back next week. He doesn't think farmwork will be challenging."

Ben looked down at Ferdy and nodded. "I hear you're a real smart one, just like your uncle," he said. "I guess I can understand why farmwork would look boring to a cub like you."

"Well," said Ferdy, "it doesn't exactly take a rocket scientist to do farmwork."

"True enough," said Ben. He had a sneaky little gleam in his eye. "I'll bet those chores would be mighty easy for you."

Ferdy yawned again. "I expect so," he said.

"In that case," said Ben, "how about doing me a favor?"

"What kind of favor?" asked Ferdy.

"I was going to show you cubs how to perform the chores," said Ben, "but my poor ol' back is kinda sore this morning. I'd be mighty grateful if you'd do the demonstratin' for me, Ferdy. That is, if you think you can handle it."

"*Of course* I can handle it," said Ferdy. "But what about my clothes?"

Farmer Ben's young nephew kept a pair of overalls at the farm for his visits. Ferdy

changed into them in the bathroom and
came back into the living room. The other
cubs giggled. For one thing, the overalls
were a couple sizes too big. For another,
Ferdy hadn't really changed his clothes.
He'd just pulled the overalls on over his
knickers and tweed jacket. Standing there
in his maroon cap, with his tweed jacket
and turtleneck showing, Ferdy didn't look
much like a farm hand.

A brisk wind was blowing from the west
as the cubs followed Farmer Ben along a

narrow path to the edge of a small plot of dark soil. "I finished planting potatoes here yesterday," said Ben. "Now it needs some fertilizer."

"What's 'fertilizer'?" asked Sister.

"It's made from manure, which has more nutrients than ordinary soil," said Farmer Ben. "The nutrients help plants grow bigger and faster."

Farmer Ben disappeared into a nearby shed and came back carrying two buckets. Some of the cubs covered their noses.

"It's not the best-smelling stuff in the world," said Ben, "but potatoes love it." He handed one of the buckets to Ferdy. "Now, son, I want you to toss a bucketful of fertilizer over each half of this plot. Go to it."

Ferdy stood at the edge of the plot, facing east. But the rising sun was in his eyes. So he walked around to the other side and faced west, away from the sun. He got a good two-handed grip on the bucket and steadied himself.

"Uh-oh," the cubs heard Farmer Ben mutter.

With all his strength, Ferdy flung the bucketful of fertilizer into the wind. And the wind flung it right back in his face.

"Ar-r-r-gh!" cried Ferdy.

"Hope you had your mouth closed!" cracked Queenie as the other cubs laughed. No one laughed harder than Trudy.

"Beginner's mistake," said Farmer Ben, handing Ferdy a rag to wipe his face with. "I'll finish up here later. Let's head for the barn."

They took a shortcut through the cow pasture. Ben often left the pasture gates open when the cows weren't outside.

"Where are the cows?" asked Lizzy, looking around.

"In the barn, waiting to be milked," said Farmer Ben. "But they left plenty of cow pies out here yesterday, so watch your step."

To one side of the barn stood the chicken coop. Ben stopped in front of it and said, "Before milking the cows, we have to feed the chickens."

The chicken coop was even smellier than

the fertilizer. *"Pew!"* said Queenie. "Go ahead, Ferdy. You'll fit right in!"

Farmer Ben picked up a large bag of chicken feed and poured the feed into a bucket. He handed the bucket to Ferdy. "Now, how hard can feeding chickens be?" he said. "Show us how to do it, my boy." He unlatched the door to the coop and held it open. "Go on, son. Git!"

Ferdy stepped inside and walked to the center of the chicken coop. He scooped a handful of feed from the bucket and said, "I believe the common phrase for such a task is 'piece of cake.'" Then he began to scatter the feed in a circle around him.

The cubs heard Farmer Ben chuckle. "That's mighty close to your body, son!" he called to Ferdy.

But it was too late. Ferdy was already surrounded by a mass of clucking, pecking chickens. What's more, in scattering feed so

close to him, he had accidentally dropped some into the cuffs of his overalls. Soon there were chickens pecking hungrily at his ankles.

"Ouch!" cried Ferdy. "Ow! Stop! Back, I say!"

The cubs laughed as Ferdy dropped the bucket and did an awkward dance to avoid his attackers. Lucky for him, the chickens went for the feed that had spilled from the fallen bucket. That gave Ferdy a chance to dash through the door and slam it behind him.

Farmer Ben patted Ferdy on the back. "We farmers have a saying," he chuckled. " 'He who drops chicken feed at his own feet soon finds himself in a peck of trouble.' Get it? *Peck* of trouble?"

"Very clever," Ferdy grumbled as the other cubs hooted and hollered.

"Cow-milking time," announced Farmer Ben.

Compared to the chicken coop, the barn didn't smell so bad. Mixed with the animal smells was a weedy odor. The cubs looked up and saw bales of hay stacked high in the hayloft.

"Now, this here is Daisy, and this is Clover," said Farmer Ben, pointing to two wooden stalls. The cows in the stalls took no notice of their visitors, but went on chewing their cud. "They're both ready for milking. Watch this."

Farmer Ben went about hooking up Daisy and Clover to two big gleaming metal machines.

"Gee," said Brother when Ben came back to the group. "I'm not sure we can handle those milking machines."

"Don't have to," said Ben, leading them

to a third stall. "Now, this here is Old Bess."
At the mention of her name, the old cow
looked back warily at the cubs. "Her milking machine is broken," Ben continued,
"and because business has been so bad
lately, I don't have the money to fix it. Old
Bess is so picky about milking that she'll
only give milk in her very own stall. So,
we've got to milk her the old-fashioned way:
by hand."

Ben handed Ferdy a half-full bucket.
"Ever seen a cow milked by hand in the
movies?" he asked.

"Certainly," said Ferdy.

"Then I guess you know all you need to," said Ben with a wink at the other cubs. "Go on, son. Git!"

Ferdy sat down on the little stool behind Old Bess and placed the bucket under her bulging udder. He grasped two nipples and pulled gently. Nothing happened.

"Better pull a little harder, son," Ben advised.

Ferdy tugged harder. But all that happened was that Old Bess looked back at Ferdy.

"Uh-oh," said Lizzy, who had a way with animals. "She looks mad."

Just then Old Bess lifted a hind leg and kicked the stool right out from under Ferdy. Ferdy fell forward and landed with his head in the bucket.

"You're sure havin' your problems with

buckets this morning, son," said Farmer Ben.

"I doubt it was my fault," said Ferdy icily. "Old Bess seems to be working no better than her milking machine."

"We'll see about that," said Farmer Ben. He took a seat on the stool and reached for Old Bess's udder. Within minutes he had a full pail of fresh milk.

"I'll bet Ferdy's had enough for one day, cubs," said Farmer Ben. "We should all thank him for being such a good sport. *And* a good teacher. You can learn a lot by seeing how *not* to do things, you know."

He turned to the defeated cub. "Since you worked extra hard today, son," he said, "I'll give an extra half-day's pay if you show up next Saturday. And I'll also give you a second chance to prove you can handle these chores. Is it a deal?"

Ferdy glanced over at Old Bess, then looked back at Ben. "Oh, all right," he said. "Deal."

Ben asked Ferdy to leave his dirty overalls in the barn and told the cubs to be back bright and early next Saturday. Then he left to check his pumpkin patch.

The sun shone brightly as the cubs trudged back across the cow pasture. A bad smell rose from Ferdy—bad enough to keep the other cubs away. But Trudy was dying to tease him. As they neared the front gate, she drifted over to him. "So, how did you like your first day of farmwork, Ferd?" she asked, holding her nose.

"I can't say I liked it at all," said Ferdy without looking at her. He walked along in glum silence for a few moments. Then he added, "But I'll admit one thing. It *wasn't* boring."

Chapter 4
A Visit from the Enemy

The following Saturday, Ferdy made good on his second chance. He tossed fertilizer *with* the wind instead of into it. He scattered chicken feed far and wide. And after a quick lesson from Farmer Ben, he even managed to get a full pail of milk out of Old Bess.

As Ferdy's skill at farmwork improved, his interest in it grew. When Farmer Ben explained to the cubs how Actual Factual

had cured last year's tomato blight by spreading a virus that attacked the blight germs, Ferdy was amazed. He looked up at Ben with wonder in his eyes and said, "But that's *ecology!*"

"Sure enough, son," said Farmer Ben. " 'Ecology' means the study of nature. And no one studies nature harder than we farmers. We have to understand how crops grow and animals breed. We need to know what diseases plants and animals get and how to prevent them. Farming isn't just a lot of dirty work, son. It's science, too."

The other cubs were also interested in farm science, but they were even more interested in the fact that Halloween was fast approaching. That made them weed the pumpkin patch with special care. They knew that the pumpkins Farmer Ben sold to folks for jack-o'-lanterns were his most important source of income for the fall. They also knew that their own parents would be among Ben's customers. And they wanted the biggest and best jack-o'-lanterns they could get.

The cubs' excitement grew even faster than the pumpkins. After just their second day of work, they had already saved enough money for Halloween costumes. They

arrived at the farm for their third week's work feeling good about getting a head start on saving money for Christmas. They were so busy feeling good, in fact, that they didn't even notice how gloomy Farmer Ben looked.

Farmer Ben had good reason to be gloomy. During the week, the fourth Beartown grocery store had closed down. That left only one store still buying Ben's goods at high prices. If the last store were to close, he would surely be forced to sell the farm. Unless, that is, Ed Hooper started paying higher prices for his goods.

As Ben and the cubs weeded the pumpkin patch that morning, a shiny new car

drove through the front gate and up to the farmhouse. Moments later, Sister looked up from her weeding and saw a bear approaching on foot across the cow pasture. "Who's *that?*" she asked Farmer Ben.

Ben gave one look and muttered, "Uh-oh. It's Ed Hooper. I'm almost afraid to ask him what he wants…"

In his three-piece suit and expensive hat, Hooper came stepping across the pasture, being very careful to avoid the cow pies.

When he reached the pumpkin patch, he walked right up to Farmer Ben and held out his hand. Ben made no move to shake it.

"As you wish, Ben," said Hooper, lowering his hand. "Five, four, three, two, one, zero!"

"What's that?" said Ben. "You going into the rocket-ship business?"

Hooper laughed. "No, Ben," he said. "That's the countdown for the number of grocery stores left in Beartown. The last one just closed down for good."

"For *your* good, maybe," Ben sneered. "Not for mine."

"That's exactly why I came over," said Hooper. "I'm worried about you. I want to assure you that I'll buy all the farm goods you've got."

Farmer Ben eyed Hooper. "Bet you're

gonna raise your prices over at the Sooper-Dooper Market," he said.

"As a matter of fact, I just did," said Hooper.

"Well, then," said Ben, "in that case, you can afford to pay us farmers higher prices for our goods, can't you?"

A little smile nudged the corners of Hooper's mouth. "I can," he said. "But I won't. My offer stands. Take it or leave it."

For a moment Farmer Ben said nothing.

Then he exploded. "I knew it! I knew it!" he roared. "I've got a broken milking machine I can't afford to fix, and I've already had to fire my farm hand! My wife had to quit the farm and take a job in town! I won't let you do this to me, Hooper! It would be an insult to all my farming ancestors if I sold my goods to you at these rotten prices! I swear I'll sell this farm before I do it!"

Farmer Ben's outburst had been so loud that some of the cubs were left holding their hands over their ears. But Ed Hooper hadn't so much as flinched.

"Well, what you do with your farm is none of my business," said Hooper.

"It darn sure isn't!" yelled Ben. "Because *your* business is robbery! You're nothin' but an old-fashioned highway robber! You put a supermarket out on the highway and use it to rob folks!"

Hooper's smug little smile got bigger. "I'm sorry you feel that way, Ben," he said. "But I can get my farm goods elsewhere. I'll be on my way now. Have a nice day, Ben."

Hooper turned to leave, but happened to glance back and see Farmer Ben reaching for a pitchfork stuck in the ground.

"Have a nice day?" Ben cried. "Don't you *dare* tell me to have a nice day!"

And with that, Farmer Ben raised his pitchfork and chased Ed Hooper into the cow pasture. Hooper dashed across the pasture toward his shiny new car. He reached the car safely, but not before stepping in three cow pies.

Chapter 5
Trudy's Great Idea

"Wow!" said Queenie. "I've never seen Farmer Ben so mad!"

The cubs were huddled in the pumpkin patch.

"Where did he go?" asked Lizzy.

"Into the house," said Ferdy. "I'll bet he's asking his ancestors for help again."

"Things sure look dark," said Brother. "Poor Ben."

"Poor Ben?" said Queenie. "What about poor *us*? If he sells the farm to one of those land developers, we'll lose our jobs!"

"All the more reason to convince him to keep the farm," said Brother.

"Convince him?" said Queenie. "How? Nothing can convince him to keep the farm except higher prices for his goods. And now there's no one left to pay high prices."

The cubs sat thinking. Suddenly Trudy said, "Yes, there is!"

"Yes, there is *what?*" asked Ferdy.

"Yes, there is someone who will pay higher prices for Farmer Ben's goods!" said Trudy. "The customers!"

"What customers?" asked Queenie.

"Hooper's customers!" said Trudy. "Farmer Ben could open a roadside market and sell his goods directly to the customers. He could sell them at much lower prices than Hooper does and still make more money than Hooper pays him."

"She's right," said Cousin Fred. "Not only

HOW ABOUT THE···
UN-HOOPER.

will Ben's goods be cheaper, but fresher, too. That will attract Hooper's customers and keep the farm going."

"What should we call the market?" said Queenie. "It has to have a snappy name. Something with real *zing!*"

"I know," said Babs. "Hooper-Busters."

"No," said Brother. "Too silly."

Barry said, "How about the...Un-Hooper."

"Nah," said Queenie. "Too dumb!"

Ferdy held up a hand to stop the discussion. "You're all forgetting about Farmer

49

Ben's pride," he said. "I hardly think he'll allow someone else to name his new market."

The other cubs agreed instantly. They all raced to the farmhouse to tell Farmer Ben about Trudy's idea.

Just as Ferdy had predicted, Ben was in the living room, gazing at the portraits of his ancestors. As Trudy breathlessly told him about her idea, a smile came to his face and a twinkle to his eye.

"That's a great idea!" he said. He looked back at the portraits. "I knew you'd come through," he told them.

"What will you name the new market, Farmer Ben?" asked Queenie. "Can you think of a good snappy name that folks will notice?"

Farmer Ben thought hard for quite a while. Finally his eyes lit up. He raised a forefinger high in the air. "I've got it!" he cried. "The perfect name!"

"What is it?" asked the cubs all at once.

Smiling broadly, Ben announced the perfect name: *Farmer Ben's Market!*

While the cubs shot puzzled looks at each other, Ferdy spoke up. "An excellent name!" he said. "So simple and direct! You certainly have a way with words, Farmer Ben."

Chapter 6
Market Madness

Farmer Ben's Market was indeed a great idea. But building it might have been quite a problem had it not been for Ben's friends and neighbors. The local lumberyard provided the lumber, on the understanding that Ben would pay for it later if the market proved a success. Papa Bear and other local carpenters teamed up to build the market,

also on the understanding that Ben would pay them later for their work.

Once built, the market was a huge success. Mrs. Ben quit her job at the fabric store to run the market with the help of the cubs working overtime. Fruits and vegetables fresh from the fields and orchards, eggs fresh from the hen, and butter fresh from the churn attracted hundreds of customers daily. Word spread quickly around

Beartown that Ed Hooper was furious about losing so many customers to Farmer Ben.

But Ed Hooper's fury did nothing to stop the flow of customers to Farmer Ben's Mar-

ket or the flow of money into the Bens' pockets. By mid-October, Farmer Ben had made enough money to rehire Jake, fix Old Bess's milking machine, and buy a brand-new tractor. And there was plenty left over to keep paying the cubs to do chores and help Mrs. Ben at the market.

Things were going so well on the farm that Farmer Ben's gloomy mood vanished. But he still wasn't quite his old jolly self. One day, when the cubs stopped by the farmhouse for some milk and cookies after work, they found Farmer Ben staring at the portraits of his ancestors again, looking very serious indeed.

"What's wrong, Farmer Ben?" asked Sister.

"Oh, hi, cubs," said Ben. "Nothing's wrong. At least, not yet. I was just hoping for some ideas from my ancestors about what to do if Hooper lowers his prices."

"You mean the way he did to drive the grocery stores out of business?" asked Cousin Fred.

"Exactly," said Ben. "If he lowers his prices far enough, he'll get most of his customers back. And if I start losing customers, I won't be able to keep up the payments on the new tractor. Or buy seed and fertilizer for next spring's crops."

"But if Hooper can run you out of business by lowering his prices," said Brother, "why hasn't he done it already?"

Farmer Ben chuckled. "Hard to say," he said. "Maybe he just can't stand the idea of one little old farmer forcing him to lower his prices."

Chapter 7
Dark Days

For a few more days, things continued to go smoothly on the farm. But when Ben and the cubs went out to the apple orchard to pick apples one fine morning, they found that every single apple was wormy.

Farmer Ben held an apple up to the sunlight and squinted at it. "Can't understand it," he said. "I sprayed the orchard with bug killer less than a week ago."

57

That was bad enough. But the very next afternoon, something else happened. Ben and the cubs went to herd the cows back into the barn and found one of the pasture gates wide open.

"Can't understand it," said Ben. "I made sure this gate was latched when I let the cows out of the barn this morning."

"Where are they?" Sister wondered.

Farmer Ben scanned the horizon. "Oh, no!" he moaned. "They're way out yonder in the onion grass! They'll be putting out onion-flavored milk for a week!"

And that wasn't the last thing that went wrong that week. The next morning was Saturday, and Ben and the cubs went out to the fields bright and early. It was time to harvest the corn, which Ben would sell to a popcorn company in Big Bear City. But as they took a shortcut across the cow pasture, Ben sniffed the air and held up a hand to stop them. "Do I smell smoke?" he said.

"Look over there!" cried Lizzy. "The cornfield must be on fire!"

Sure enough, an orange glow was visible in the distance. Sooty black smoke rose from it into the dawn sky. Ben and the cubs broke into a run. By the time they reached the cornfield, the fire was almost out.

Ben gazed grimly at his smoking cornfield. All over the charred ground lay thousands of ears of corn. The fire hadn't destroyed them. It had done a different kind of damage.

"This is terrible!" said Ben. "I can't sell my corn to the popcorn company if it's *already popped!*"

"How did the fire start?" Babs wondered.

As Farmer Ben thought, his expression got grimmer. "Wormy apples, a pasture gate left open, and now this," he said. "It can't be a coincidence."

"Do you mean someone set the fire on purpose?" asked Queenie.

"Yep," said Ben. "And left the pasture gate open. And hosed the bug spray off those apples."

"Well, at least you still have your prize pumpkins," said Brother. "Won't selling them get you all the way through Thanksgiving?"

But Farmer Ben didn't look relieved. "My pumpkins!" he cried. "We'd better check them right away!"

They hurried to the pumpkin patch. What they saw there made their hearts sink. The pumpkins were still there. But they were all twisted into weird, spooky shapes.

"My beautiful pumpkins!" moaned Farmer Ben. "My most important fall crop! This is a disaster!"

"What happened to them?" asked Sister.

"Pumpkin blight," said Ben. "Could have been an accident. But I doubt it. There are at least a dozen kinds of pumpkin blight, and not a single one has hit a Beartown area farm this year."

"Hmm," said Ferdy. "Kind of makes you think someone got hold of some blight germs and let them loose in the pumpkin patch."

"Who do you think did it, Ben?" asked Barry.

"Well, I've only got one enemy in all Bear Country," said Farmer Ben. "I always knew Ed Hooper was a lowdown creep. But I never thought he'd stoop *this* low."

Chapter 8
A Brilliant Plan

Farmer Ben called the police right away, and Chief Bruno came out to the farm to investigate the crimes. The chief found no evidence that pointed to Ed Hooper. But he did find something interesting when he contacted the Big Bear City Police to see if there had been similar crimes recently in that area. There hadn't. But someone *had*

stolen several test tubes containing pumpkin blight germs from the Farm Science Laboratory at Big Bear University. Unfortunately, that crime hadn't been solved yet, either.

Catching the criminal would have put a stop to the crimes, of course. But it wouldn't have helped Farmer Ben. His three most important fall crops were no longer fit for sale. He told Mrs. Ben that there was no way the farm could recover from the loss. Now he wouldn't be able to keep up with the payments on the new tractor. And by mid-November, there wouldn't even be enough money left in their account at Great Grizzly National Bank to put food on the Ben table. Mrs. Ben offered to go back to work at the fabric store, but Ben said her wages there weren't enough to save the farm. And he was right. They had no choice now but to sell the farm to a land developer.

Farmer Ben looked like a beaten bear as he announced his decision to the cubs gathered in his living room. And then, with a huge lump in his throat, he turned to the portraits on the wall and apologized to his ancestors for letting them down. It was a sad moment indeed.

The cubs were stunned as they walked homeward. They didn't want to lose their jobs. But they were more worried about the Bens' loss than their own. Especially Ferdy. Ferdy had come a long way in his respect for farming. Every day since his first day of work, he and Farmer Ben had been discussing the science of farming: how to increase milk yields, how to improve the flavor of tomatoes, how to fight new types of blight. Ferdy and Ben had even planned

farm research projects together. They had become as close friends as a cub and a grownup can.

Ferdy was convinced that selling the farm would make Farmer Ben unhappy for the rest of his life. He knew it was time to come to his friend's aid. So he asked the other cubs to go to the Burger Bear with him for a brainstorming session. Together they

would search their minds for ways to raise money for the Ben farm.

Over shakes in their favorite booth, the cubs brainstormed their way to a truly brilliant plan. On the night before Halloween they would hold a grand Halloween Festival at the farm. They would charge folks ten dollars each to get in. There would be a big cookout. But the main attraction would be the Haunted Hayride. Customers riding atop bales of hay on a tractor-pulled cart

would squeal and shriek at spooky sounds coming from hidden loudspeakers and at cubs in scary costumes along the way.

Ferdy had an idea for using holograms to make imaginary ghosts in the night sky during the hayride. He explained how holograms can make objects appear to float in space through the use of laser beams, mirrors, and lenses. He would get help from his uncle Actual Factual, who had been studying holograms lately.

The cubs also came up with great ideas about how to make money from the recent disasters. They would grind the wormy apples into Ben's Best Cider, which would be sold at the festival for ten dollars a gallon. The onion milk would become Mrs. Ben's Secret Recipe Cream of Onion Soup, at eight dollars a quart. They would sell a

new Halloween specialty: popcorn-on-the-cob. And they would charge six dollars apiece for their Super Spooky Monster Pumpkins.

It was a surefire plan. Ferdy did some quick calculations and showed that the Halloween Festival could raise enough money to pay off the new tractor, keep the milking machines in good working order, buy seed and fertilizer for next spring's crops, and also put food on the Ben table and keep the farmhouse heated through the winter. In the meantime, Farmer Ben could continue selling his dairy products. And by late spring, he would be ready to reopen Farmer Ben's Market.

After another round of shakes to celebrate their new plan, the cubs hurried back to the farm to tell Farmer Ben all about it.

Chapter 9
A Farmer's Pride Revisited

"Well, Farmer Ben," said Ferdy eagerly, "what do you think of our plan?"

Sitting in his easy chair, Ben had listened carefully as Ferdy described the plan for the Halloween Festival. The cubs had expected Ben's gloomy expression to change when he heard the plan. But now there was no smile on his face or twinkle in his eye.

"I don't like it," he said.

The cubs were shocked.

"Why not?" asked Ferdy. "What's wrong with it?"

"It's show business, not farming," said Ben. "Maybe you'd like me to get up and tap-dance for the folks, too." He looked up at the portraits of his ancestors. "I know what Ben Ezra, Ben Abner, and Ben Noah would think of the Halloween Festival. They'd hate it."

Ferdy said, "But it would save the—"

"Tap-dancin', that's all it is!" Ben snapped. "My dear old papa, Ben Noah, had a term for this kind of non-farmin' foolishness that farmers get involved in. He called it 'tap-dancin' on cow pies.' "

Ferdy might have looked hurt if he hadn't been thinking so hard. What should he do? He could tell Mrs. Ben about the plan.

Maybe she could get Farmer Ben to change his mind. But he didn't want to start a big argument between Farmer and Mrs. Ben.

Suddenly Ferdy's eyes lit up. "Of course, we respect your decision, Farmer Ben," he said. "I'd like to make one last request, if I may. Would you allow us cubs to sleep in the barn tomorrow night? Sort of our way of saying good-bye to the farm."

"A sleepover?" said Ben. "Why, sure. After everything you cubs have done for Mrs. Ben and me, it's the least I can do."

"Then perhaps you'll grant me another last request," said Ferdy. "Would you and the cubs wait while I go home and get my camera and tripod? I'd like to take a group photo right here in the living room."

"I'd be honored," said Farmer Ben. "Go on, son. Git!"

Trudy went with Ferdy so she could carry

the camera while he carried the tripod. As they headed down the drive to the front gate, Trudy said, "A sleepover and group photo are wonderful ideas, Ferd. Very sweet."

"Sweet has nothing to do with it," said Ferdy. "I think I know how to save the Halloween Festival—and, thus, the farm!"

Chapter 10
Ghosts of Farmers Past

The next day on the farm was a quiet one as Farmer Ben made plans to sell his cows and chickens. Several other farmers made appointments to come to the farm with their animal doctors to examine Ben's livestock. As soon as Ben found a new home for his cows and chickens, he would sell the farm to a land developer.

That evening, after dinner, the cubs gathered in the barn with their flashlights and sleeping bags. They were usually happy on sleepovers, but not this time. For hours they talked softly about all their fond memories of working on the farm. Finally, long after the cows had settled down in their stalls, the cubs switched off their flashlights and went to sleep.

Sometime later, Lizzy was awakened by the cows stirring in their stalls. She woke up Sister, who was sleeping beside her.

"What's up?" asked Sister, rubbing her eyes.

"Something's upsetting the cows," whispered Lizzy. "Maybe Ed Hooper is snooping around again. Do you think we should investigate?"

But before Sister could answer, something happened that made Lizzy shout loud enough to wake up the rest of the cubs.

"Look!" she cried. "Up in the hayloft!"

Three glowing faces had appeared side by side. They seemed to float in the air, just above the bales of hay.

"Burglars!" said Barry.

"*Hay* burglars?" Queenie wondered.

Suddenly a wailing sound filled the barn. *"Who-o-o! Who-o-o! WHO-O-O-O-O!"*

Sister grabbed Lizzy's arm. "Those aren't barn owls!" she moaned. "I'm scared!"

"I'll go get Farmer Ben!" said Brother.

"Wait!" said Cousin Fred. "Haven't we seen those faces before?"

Just then the latch on the barn door clicked open and Farmer Ben came rushing in with a flashlight in one hand and a pitchfork in the other. "What's going on in here?"

he demanded. Then he saw the glowing faces. "What in *tarnation*...?"

At that moment the faces spoke. "*We ...are...the...Ben...ancestors...*" they wailed in low, wobbly voices that seemed to come from another world.

Farmer Ben let out a gasp. "Ben Ezra! Ben Abner! Ben Noah! Why have you come back?"

Now only one of the voices spoke. "To tell you that you are making a great mistake!"

"By selling the farm?" asked Ben.

"Y-E-E-S-S-S!" said the voice. "This is

your papa speaking! You must hold the Halloween Festival!"

Farmer Ben was shaking in awe. "But, Papa," he said, "you ordered me never to tap-dance on cow pies…"

"Don't be a slave to my orders, son!" said the voice. "You must try new things!"

Farmer Ben gulped. "Is that an order?" he asked weakly.

"YES!" boomed the voice. "Now go plan the Halloween Festival! Go on, son! Git!"

With that, the glowing faces faded until only flashlight beams lit the barn.

Farmer Ben thrust his pitchfork into the dirt floor of the barn. "My ancestors have spoken, cubs," he said. "I was wrong about selling the farm. We *will* hold the Halloween Festival!"

The cubs let out a cheer in unison: "Hip, hip, hooRAY!"

Chapter 11
The Secret of the Ghosts

"Ghosts!" said Sister when Farmer Ben had gone back to the farmhouse. "I can't believe I saw real ghosts!"

"Amazing!" said Babs. "I must be dreaming! Somebody pinch me!"

"Wait a second," said Fred, looking

around. "What happened to Ferdy and Trudy?"

"They're gone!" said Queenie.

"No, we're not," said two voices. "We're up here."

The cubs looked up to see Ferdy and Trudy climbing down the hayloft ladder. Ferdy had a box under one arm, and Trudy was carrying something that looked like a laptop computer attached to a microphone.

"Did you see the ghosts?" asked Sister.

"We didn't just see them," said Ferdy. "We *made* them."

"What do you mean, you made them?" asked Brother.

Ferdy put down his box and took something from it. "This is a hologram of Farmer Ben's ancestors. We made it from a photographic plate in my uncle's laboratory at the Bearsonian." He lifted more objects from the box. "Just now we projected the holo- gram image in the hayloft, using these lenses and this laser."

"Wow!" said Cousin Fred. "But how did you make the faces so real? They looked just like the portraits in Farmer Ben's living room."

"Simple," said Ferdy. He took a snapshot from the breast pocket of his tweed jacket and held it up for all to see. It was the group photo he had taken the day before in the Bens' living room. Farmer Ben stood at the far left, with Mrs. Ben at the far right.

In between them were the cubs all in a row, including Ferdy, who had taken the photo using a timer. Also between Ben and his wife, but above and behind the shorter cubs, were the portraits of Ben Ezra, Ben Abner, and Ben Noah.

"My uncle has recently discovered how to make holograms from ordinary photographs," Ferdy continued. "That's why I arranged us so that the portraits would appear in the group photo."

"Awesome!" said Queenie. "Ferdy, you're a genius!"

"That's what all the girls say," said Ferdy. "Boys, too, actually."

"But how did you get the ancestors to talk?" asked Barry.

Trudy patted the machine she was holding. "Ferdy did all the talking," she said, "but *I* ran the voice synthesizer."

"I borrowed it from my uncle," said Ferdy. "It can do all sorts of weird things to your voice. Even make it sound like several voices at once."

"Why didn't you tell us about this?" asked Sister. "You scared the heck out of me with those ghosts!"

"I wanted your natural reactions to the ghosts," Ferdy explained. "I was afraid that any bad acting on your part would make Farmer Ben suspect it was all a trick."

"And it worked," said Trudy. "Farmer Ben didn't suspect a thing."

"This is terrific!" cried Queenie. "We can make all kinds of spooky holograms for the Haunted Hayride!"

"Oh, no," said Ferdy. "I'll admit that was my intention earlier. But now we can't do it."

"Why not?" asked Queenie.

"When Farmer Ben sees the holograms at the hayride," said Ferdy, "he might realize that the ghosts of his ancestors were made in the same way. And Farmer Ben must never know that we tricked him into saving the farm. Even though it was for his own good."

The cubs agreed to keep the secret of the ghosts. Then, after one more "Hip, hip, hooray!" for Ferdy and Trudy, they all curled up in their sleeping bags for a good night's sleep.

Chapter 12
Hayride Mischief

Now that Farmer Ben was in favor of the Halloween Festival, he threw himself into the preparations with all his heart. He advertised on radio stations and in newspapers as far away as Big Bear City. He helped Papa Bear build dozens of picnic tables for the grand cookout. And he drove all around the countryside looking for good deals on ground beef for burgers so he

wouldn't have to pay the high prices at
Hooper's Sooper-Dooper Market. Mrs. Ben
worked just as hard making gallon after gallon of Ben's Best Cider and quart after
quart of her Secret Recipe Cream of Onion
Soup.

The Bens had a lot of help, too. Not only
did Papa Bear donate his labor, but the
cubs worked long hours without pay to
build pop-up and pop-out spooks for the
Haunted Hayride. They also donned their
trick-or-treat costumes and rehearsed jump-

ing out from behind trees along the hayride route. Biff Bruin donated dozens of paper lanterns to light the festival. And Chief Bruno offered to patrol the farm during the festival in order to discourage rowdies and troublemakers.

At last the big night arrived. Bears came from far and wide. There were so many that Mrs. Ben worried there might not be enough food. Many of the cub visitors came in their trick-or-treat costumes. Even some of the grownups wore costumes.

At dusk, as soon as the festival opened,

Mrs. Ben started serving burgers with the help of Papa and Mama Bear. When it was completely dark, Farmer Ben announced the first run of the long-awaited Haunted Hayride. Excited cubs and grownups piled onto the hay-filled cart. Pulled by the new tractor with Farmer Ben at the wheel, the cart set off on its journey around the farm.

Along the way, painted dragons and vampires popped up from behind rocks and bushes. Costumed ghosts and goblins

dashed out from behind trees. Loudspeakers hidden in trees and in the hayloft of the barn filled the night air with spooky wails and moans. The riders shrieked and squealed in fear and delight.

Then, all of a sudden, someone came running toward the hayride from the direction of the front gate. It was Chief Bruno.

He stopped right in front of Farmer Ben's tractor and held up a hand. "Halt!" he shouted. "Don't go another inch!"

"What's wrong, Chief?" asked Farmer Ben.

"Someone's been messing with the hay cart," said the chief. "Take a look at the left rear wheel."

Farmer Ben climbed down from the tractor to examine the cart wheel. Sure enough, it was loose. So loose, in fact, that it was about to come off.

"Tarnation!" cried Farmer Ben. "My riders could have been hurt! Not just scrapes and bruises, either! Broken bones!" He turned back to Chief Bruno. "Who did this?"

Now Officer Marguerite arrived on the scene, accompanied by a tall bear in a pirate costume. "Here's your culprit," said Marguerite.

"Hooper!" roared Ben. "It's you!"

"I've had my eye on him all evening," said Bruno. "He was one of the first to get here, and he looked nervous. At dinner, he kept looking over at the hay cart. That made me real suspicious. So, when he got up from dinner, I asked him to come over under one of the paper lanterns so I could get a good look at his great costume. Meanwhile, Marguerite sneaked up behind him and pulled off his mask. As soon as I saw who it was, I knew he was up to no good."

"I could have been ruined, Chief," said Farmer Ben. "This bear is a menace to society!"

"Shut up, you dumb farmer!" growled Hooper.

"*You* shut up, Hooper!" snapped Chief Bruno. "You're lucky you confessed. And not a moment too soon." He turned back to Farmer Ben. "I told him that if he'd done anything to wreck the festival, he'd better admit it while there was still time. He got real scared and said he'd paid a Big Bear City criminal to come out last night and crowbar that wheel loose. He must have realized that if anyone got hurt on the hayride, the law would be a lot tougher on him. As it is, he'll do some time in Bear Country Prison. Cuff him, Marguerite!"

While Chief Bruno led Ed Hooper to the squad car, Farmer Ben busied himself tightening the loose cart wheel. Soon the hayride was back in action. It finished not only that first run without a mishap, but many more before the night was through.

Chapter 13
Business or Revenge?

The Halloween Festival had been a huge success, and now trick-or-treating was only a few hours away. You'd think that Brother and Sister Bear would be on top of the world.

But they weren't. As the afternoon wore on, they stayed in their room talking about the trick that Ferdy and Trudy had played on Farmer Ben. Had it been the right thing to do? Brother and Sister weren't so sure. Mama and Papa had taught them to tell the truth, especially to their elders.

Finally, they decided they should tell Mama what had happened. They went downstairs and found her in the living room, reading a magazine.

"Hmm," said Mama when the cubs had finished telling the story of the amazing hologram "ghosts." "I see why you're worried about it. Ordinarily, pretending to be someone's ancestors would be cruel."

"But what about this time?" asked Sister.

"Well, let's think it through," said Mama. "Farmer Ben was about to sell his farm, and the Halloween Festival would save it. Ben wanted very much to keep the farm. The only thing that stood in his way was his belief that his ancestors would disapprove of the festival. If Ferdy could persuade Farmer Ben that his ancestors approved of the festival, Ben would save his farm without feeling as if he had gone against the wishes of his ancestors. Now, what do *you* think was right, cubs?"

Sister didn't have to think long. "When you put it that way, Mama," she said, "it sounds like Ferdy and Trudy did the right thing."

"I agree," said Brother.

"As a matter of fact," said Mama, "so do I."

Just then Papa came bursting through the front door with the afternoon paper. "Look at this!" he said, holding up the paper. The front-page headline read: SOOPER-DOOPER MARKET HAS NEW OWNERS.

Papa read the article aloud. " 'Ed

LOOK AT THIS!

BEARNEWS
SOOPER-
DOOPER
MARKET
HAS NEW
OWNERS

Hooper, faced with lawyers' bills, fines, and probably jail time, has sold Hooper's Sooper-Dooper Market, located on Bear Country Highway near Birder's Woods. The new owners are the former owners of five Beartown grocery stores that closed recently. They have announced that they will immediately lower the prices they charge their customers. At the same time, they will increase the prices they pay local farmers for their goods.' "

"Yay!" cried Sister. "That solves all of Farmer Ben's problems!"

"Wait, there's more," said Papa, running a finger down the column of newsprint. " 'The Big Bear City Police reported this morning that a worker at Big Bear University's Farm Science Laboratory has admitted that Ed Hooper paid him to steal several test tubes containing pumpkin blight. The

OUTTA SIGHT!

results of tests on Farmer Ben's pumpkins have just been announced. They show that the blight that attacked Ben's pumpkin patch is exactly the same kind that Ed Hooper got from the Farm Science Laboratory.'"

"Outta sight!" shouted Brother, pumping a fist in the air. "They got Hooper for the pumpkin-blight caper!"

Papa put down the paper and shook his head. "There's one thing about all this I just don't understand," he said. "Ed Hooper could have run Farmer Ben's Market out of business by lowering his prices. Sure, he would have lost money for a few weeks, but it would have been a lot safer than damaging Ben's crops. Same thing with the Halloween Festival. Hooper didn't have to ruin it. All he had to do was wait until Farmer Ben's Market got going again, then run him out of business by lowering prices. But it seems that Hooper didn't just want to run Ben out of business. He wanted to embarrass him. He wanted to destroy Ben's reputation, and he wanted to be there to watch it happen. It wasn't just business. It was *personal.* I wonder why."

No sooner had Brother started thinking about Papa's question than a picture floated into his mind's eye. It was a picture of a terrified Ed Hooper running wildly through Farmer Ben's cow pasture, stepping in cow pies, with Ben chasing him.

"No need to wonder, Papa," said Brother with a grin. "I think I know the answer."

Stan and Jan Berenstain began writing and illustrating books for children in the early 1960s, when their two young sons were beginning to read. That marked the start of the best-selling Berenstain Bears series. Now, with more than one hundred books in print, videos, television shows, and even Berenstain Bears attractions at major amusement parks, it's hard to tell where the Bears end and the Berenstains begin!

Stan and Jan make their home in Bucks County, Pennsylvania, near their sons—Leo, a writer, and Michael, an illustrator—who are helping them with Big Chapter Books stories and pictures. They plan on writing and illustrating many more books for children, especially for their four grandchildren, who keep them well in touch with the kids of today.